Venus and

Written By

Indiana Phoenix

Table of Contents

For Tony.
Thank you for always encouraging me.
For Vinnic and Veila.
Thank you for inspiring me daily.

A Map of Faerie

~An Agreement~

Once upon a time in a dreamy and distant land filled with music and fireflies and creatures of all types, there lived a fae, but not the kind with wings, or at least, not yet. She was the kind who walked on two feet and blessed the earth around her, making the soil rich and the fruit sweet, the trees tall and the flowers resilient. She could also do a slew of other mystical things, and she could curse those who brought harm to the earth if she chose. Tonight, was one of those nights where she chose a curse.

Her shadowy skin somehow reflected every color in the room and her thick, snowy hair shimmered in the yellow lights. Half of her hair was pulled up into a thick bun, and the other half in two fat braids which hung about her collarbone, tied off by two brass cuffs. They tinged about as she moved.

She adjusted the snug wooden crown sitting on her head as she scurried through the solid gold palace halls, lined with tapestry, and adorned with luxurious furnishings, all handwoven by weaving spiders. The palace bustled with guests and servants. They laughed and mingled and flirted and argued, all dressed in long robes, polished jewels, giant headdresses, scanty tunics, or hardly any clothing at all. No one noticed a fae creature in there that night, the night of a masque ball. But normally, the fae were reclusive and thus a rare sight.

Tonight, Venus went unnoticed even in her own attire, or lack thereof, which was nothing more than a thin green rope, given to her by the Spider Queen when she was born, crisscrossed around her torso and green thong underwear. Fae don't find clothing necessary as they're immune to the weather and rarely enter battle. So, she walked through the halls, being shoved into the kitchen, and being mistaken for a server, all much to her advantage.

The kitchen was lit up with candles like a bonfire and smelled of pork roast and sweaty humans. It was packed with servants of all sizes,

bustling around, yelling at each other, and hurrying in and out the swinging wooden doors. Venus's blood pressure shot through the roof at the sight- that was until someone handed her a great, golden tray with a pitcher of wine and two royal goblets on it.

"Take this to the czar." She was commanded.

Fate favored her on this night in her endeavors and she didn't hesitate. Her night of revenge on the man who'd either killed or stolen the Monkey Prince- whom she'd admired from afar- killed the Fae King- whom she respected greatly- and destroyed an entire forest to build his palace, was going exactly as planned. She hurried through the halls, squeezing through the mass of spatially unaware guests. As she went, she cursed the wine, turning it quite rancid, though not in taste or smell. It would be poisonous to the body though and kill the czar slowly and painfully, an ailment with no medicine to cure him.

Inside the great dining hall, where the heart of the party was, and where the czar sat on his pile of cushions, surrounded by nobles and minstrels, she would find her sweet revenge. The crowd roared with laughter and even more chaos filled this room than the kitchen. Filled with elven men, fae women, dwarves, and humans alike, it proved a lively swarm of guests indeed. She wove her way through, more slowly now as a train of dancers with masks filed through. She finally saw the czar once they passed. She glowered at his pale skin and thin, blonde eyebrows that looked all too strange on his prominent brow bone. His thick, and strangely black, mustache moved around as he spoke and laughed and angered her even more. But what angered her most was the scar across his cheek and nose; he'd received it from the Fae King in a bloody battle not long ago. Now Venus stood there, ready to avenge his death.

She put on her act and began to approach him with a friendly smile. As she did, the czar leaned over to his wife, taking her spoon, and stealing a bite of sorbet. She said something in his ear, making him laugh. He inhaled the tiny spoon in the middle of taking his bite and laughing. The spoon lodged in his throat. He erupted in a massive coughing fit. His wife wailed in panic. The commotion drew nearly the whole crowd in a wave of chaos, all thronging in to either help or see what was happening. Venus immediately drew back, dropping the wine on the stone flooring beneath her with a resounding clatter.

No one noticed as they were all fixated on the czar. Several other dishes dropped in a panic. She could barely see what was going on, but as the royal guard, clanging in their silver armor, pushed their way through and gave her a window, she saw the czar slouched over, his face quite purple and his body quite still. She watched as they tried to aid him to no avail, and finally was declared dead.

Venus wasn't quite sure why, but she wasn't satisfied. She wanted to be the cause of his demise and now the only culprit was a tiny, silver, sorbet

 spoon. How could she reasonably say she had avenged the Fae King's death when she'd had nothing to do with it? Her face flushed and anger washed over her. She turned and ran out, pushing away from the crowd and leaping out an open window. She landed softly on the dirt below her, firmly packed from many feet having passed over it. The warm air of a southern summer blew in her face, and the humidity stuck to her bare skin. She decided to keep running, nearly flying over the lush green grass of the royal yards and out into the golden wheat fields. In the moonlight, they were

nothing but wavy shadows to which she ran. She ran until she no longer saw a point, as no one was really after her.

She only ran to escape the anger of her failure. She crossed a path, worn by carriages and hooves, then came into a vineyard, walking into one of the rows and feeling the freshly weeded soil soften beneath her feet.

Fireflies blazed here and there, glowing brightly for one moment and disappearing the next. The grape leaves trembled in the wind which hummed as it passed through all the cracks and openings in the trellises. Venus picked a few of the abnormally large grapes and ate them as she went, already quite calm despite her failure, the place filled with great peace. She blessed the soil with great health. A golden glow radiated about the ground and it sparkled. As it glowed, it ignited the ground enough to reveal a pair of monkey-like feet in front of her. She stopped, following them up.

Hairy legs and a perfectly balanced combination of monkey and man wore a crimson skirt thing that tied in the front with a thick rope- she wasn't sure if it was a skirt or shorts to be quite honest. Silver cuffs decorated his wrists and obnoxiously giant wooden beads hung about his bare chest. He held a marble staff in his right hand.

"Who are you?" she asked, finally looking at his face. "Who am I?" he sighed, clearly a question he'd heard many times, and hopped up on the wooden fence which the vines clung to.

His deep voice was no less devious than a child's. Venus stared up at him cluelessly. His eyes creased with a smile, though his mouth never moved. He stroked his golden beard. He seemed a playful man, despite his harsh features, and she already knew she couldn't trust him, but not because he was bad. Just because he might untie her rope, steal her crown, or trip her into a puddle, or something else silly and annoying.

"I think it's obvious." He replied after a while, revealing a real and very coy smile, his beady eyes glimmering in the yellow glow that slowly dimmed.

"I don't think so." She stated. "I've never seen or heard of your kind before."

"I'll give you three guesses."

"And if I get it wrong?" she asked.

"I get one of the hairs from your head."

"No. I won't play your game then." She replied, walking away. Before she knew it, she felt the smallest prick on her scalp, though quite painful. She whipped around to find the monkey man holding a hair in his hands.

"Give it back!" she shouted in alarm, diving for it.

He moved all too quickly, propelling right over her with his staff. Even though he was great in size and build, he moved as light on his feet as a small faerie. She leaped for him again, but he tripped her, as she'd already anticipated, she fell on the dirt, thankfully not in a puddle. She sat up and turned around to face him, just in time to see him wrapping it around his middle finger like a ring. It glowed white for a bit, then pink, then dimmed. It never went out.

"That wasn't fair." She huffed, her throat tightening.

"Neither is walking away." He retorted.

"You made a condition I couldn't accept."

"And yet here I am. A hair from your head."

"You stole it!" she jumped up. "That's dishonorable to say the least!"

She took a step forward but he merely extended his staff, stopping her with the end of it. She looked down at the butt which pressed to her sternum. Three silver bells hung from the staff; however, they made no noise. They were scuffed and bent open without beads in the center.

"Your bells are broken." She observed.

"Fix them and I'll tell you who I am." He replied.

"I can't. I don't have any beads."

"I know. You must retrieve the beads from Baba Yaga and then you can. She took them from me. Now I'm not myself. She owns a vital piece of me and I want it back."

"Baba Yaga?" she scoffed. "Absolutely not, you lunatic. Just buy some new ones and enjoy your evening."

She turned away once more and walked off. "I have your hair." She heard him from behind.

"I know." She grumbled under her breath and kept going. "I don't care. I won't help you. Now be gone before I curse you."

He watched her for a bit, then disappeared. Venus sighed in relief as she heard him leave. She fumed. She must now do a task for him. She was bound. Ignoring the weight of the tie, she kept walking through the dark, refusing to help him. She furrowed her brows as she smelled smoke and so turned around. The orange glow of flames lit up the sky as the vineyard began burning up. Her heart sank in her chest, but she didn't have time to grieve. She turned and ran away from the growing flames as they neared, the heat already on her skin.

"Stop this nonsense right now!" she shouted over her shoulder, hoping he was still close enough to hear her.

"Fix the bells!" the monkey man shouted back from somewhere in the fire.

She yipped in fright, jumping to the side as flames bit at her skin.

"You have to help me!" his voice came again, now from one row over.

"Help yourself! You can make fire; you'll be fine without me!"

"I didn't do this! You brought it on yourself when you said no. Besides, there's a shield around me, I can't find her. She cast a spell on me but without the beads I can't break it."

Venus let out an exasperated huff as she ran. One of the trellises fell in front of her, blocking her path. She jumped back, a wave of sparks hitting her in the face. She was trapped all around, but even as a fae, there was nothing she could do about the fire. She was still young in terms of fae and didn't yet have all her gifts. She looked up. The monkey man extended his staff to her. She took it and he pulled her up, sweeping her above the flames and tossing her out onto the grass beside the vineyard. He jumped down beside her.

"Say you'll help me." He urged her, squatting down beside her.

"Fine! I'll help you!"

The fire immediately subsided, burning slowly now, and reducing to nothing but coals. She stared at it with wide eyes, mortified. She'd never refused a bind before now so had never paid the consequence.

"That was completely unnecessary!" she erupted, blaming him. "If you hadn't stolen my hair this vineyard would still be here!"

"It is still here. And with your blessing, it will grow back in a few days. Even better than before."

She clenched her jaw in anger. "Is that your only request?"

"Do I get more?"

"No!" she barked. "Unless you want bad luck for the rest of your life."

"Then yes. Get my beads. I'm nobody without them."

"Under one condition."

"That's not how it works." He smirked and raised an eyebrow. "You fix the bells. I tell you who I am. You're bound until you finish or die."

He raised his hand, reminding her again of the glowing hair around his finger. She sighed. The monkey man leaned forward and picked up a few of the leaves that hadn't been burned, then stuck them in her hair behind her crown. As the stems were buried among her hair to keep them in place, they seemed to glow a tiny bit, drawing life from the magic of the fae. Two grapes grew from their vines. The monkey man plucked one and ate it.

"Hm. Just as I thought. Even better than before." He observed, then attempted to assure her. "I will uphold my word."

"Promise." She narrowed her eyes.

"I don't make promises." He replied wistfully. "I might die before you succeed."

Then, with a point of his staff, he disappeared into a portal that zipped shut behind him, leaving nothing but a few orange sparks and golden hairs to fall on the ground. She reached down and picked the hairs up, analyzing them. They were nothing but golden hairs, about three inches in length. She didn't know that though and kept them just in case. She also just liked them, and so weaved them into her own braid, then got up and disappeared into the forest.

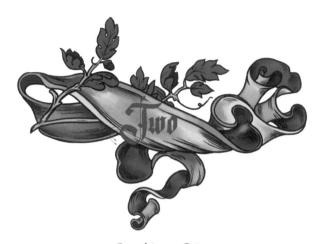

~A Heavy Name~

Venus trudged along, her journey to find the wild and horribly deceitful Baba Yaga weighing on her mind. She'd never met her, but every tale of her was true. Even the embellished ones weren't far from the truth. At one point, she was a kind young woman, a healer, and a friend of the earth. As she aged, something changed, and no one knew what. They speculated and created tales but none were ever correct. Now her skin wrinkled and darkened and so did her heart. Venus knew nothing of how to find her, except go a bit north to a mountain where the sun never quite rose and never quite set either. She wondered how she'd find her. She thought to start by finding her house. A house on legs that constantly moved around the mountain though. It'd be hard to miss, but also hard to catch or follow.

Acres of farmland slowly turned into open plains of grass and wildflowers, buzzing with the sound of bees, and screaming cicada. Bushy woods surrounded the plain, but quite far out in the distance. She sneezed at the abrupt cloud of pollen wafting up her nose and immediately decided to bless the bees, hoping they might take more pollen elsewhere. All was quiet in the field, save for the bugs, and she quite forgot about her journey and the monkey man, plucking the grapes which constantly replaced themselves from her hair, and eating them absentmindedly.

After walking through the field for some time, a layer of yellow pollen covered her skin so she meandered into a section of the field where a patch of pine trees grew, and the grass dissipated into a layer of pine needles. Underneath, she dusted herself off with a great eruption of sneezes then looked around.

Inside the cluster of pines, she found the Stream of Silver Waters, which she had often visited before in her youth, and so knelt to drink from it. As she did, a rather unwelcomed monkey man appeared from his portal, coming up from out of the water and splashing her in the face. She screamed and fell backward as he leaped out, crouching over her, also immediately erupting into a sneezing fit upon inhaling the cloud of pollen surrounding her. She watched in shock, trying to recall where she'd met him. He seemed familiar, but a dream type of familiar. Once he'd regained his composure, he spoke.

"How's your progress going? Any closer to Baba Yaga?"

"What? Get off me!" she spat, shoving him away. "And bless you."

He landed lightly, sitting in a squat and leaning on his staff. "You forgot, didn't you?" She suddenly remembered him, her quest, and the hair he had stolen.

"Of course I forgot! Fae aren't meant for great quests! My only point in life is to make the flowers grow!"

"Maybe so... but the fae are quite untouchable."

"Maybe a trickster fae. But I'm not one."

"What are you?"

"The kind that keeps to myself."

"Even so, Baba Yaga wouldn't harm you. She knows it's terrible luck to harm a fae."

"That didn't stop the czar." Venus grumbled, finally taking a drink of water.

"He's human, what does he know? He got what was coming to him."

"You already heard?" she whipped around to look at him, but he had moved up to a tree above her. She leaned back and looked up to see him hanging by his legs above her.

"I heard he choked on a sorbet spoon. What a way to go… not to mention the faeries have already started overrunning the palace, eating the food and driving out the "nobles" … pious lot they are." He chided, reaching out and booping her nose. "I should thank them for doing what I've been wanting to do for a while now."

She batted him away. He let go of the limb and dropped down, twisting, and landing on his feet in front of her. He sat and reached to the back of his rope belt, pulling out a long, thin smoking pipe and stuffing it with tobacco from the pouch on his waist, as well as a match, striking it on a rock and lighting the tobacco. He sat there for a minute, enjoying his tobacco and blowing a smoke ring. As Venus watched the ring, it reminded her of the ring of sparks that he traveled through and realized she'd only ever heard of people wishing they had the ability, and never of anyone actually having it.

"Where'd you get your power to teleport?"

"Baba Yaga." He replied as he inhaled.

"In exchange for what?"

"It's a mystery even to those I tell. But if you get me those beads all can become clear as this stream."

"So you made a deal with her that you're now trying to go back on? And you've roped me into it."

"Haired, actually." He replied smartly, tapping his middle finger on the pipe as he puffed.

She glared at him. He sat there, puffing, rather unbothered.

"What will you do in the meantime? Sit and wait?"

"What else would I do?" he chuckled. "I told you. There's a shield spell preventing me from ever finding her. I could walk straight past her house and never find it. She's quite powerful."

"Which is why I'd like to forget my quest."

"I won't let you." The monkey man smiled and grabbed the gigantic beads from his neck and slipped them over her head.

She fell back onto her bottom. "They're too heavy!"

"Good. Now you can't possibly forget."

"I can't carry these. Do you have anything else?"

"I could give you my belt… no. My pants would fall off." He thought aloud. "My staff would be far too heavy as well."

"How about a name? A name is heavy enough."

"I think I'll pass. Everyone knows you never give your name to a fae."

She gave him a sly smile and a side-eye. His own eyes glittered knowingly.

"Do you have a baby?" she tried. "I love babies."

"So you are a trickster." He chided.

"Are you accusing me of lying?"

"I would never!" He gasped. "But you can't fool me, love... and no, I don't have a baby."

She let out a small hmph! Then crossed her legs. He gave a thoughtful hum and took the gigantic necklace back, thinking of what name he could give her.

"How bout I give you a name? What about Samas? Since your hair is golden like the sun." Venus suggested.

"I like that... Very well... Hold out your hand."

Venus did so, opening her palm to him. He grabbed her wrist in one hand, and with the other, plucked a hair from his head. When he did, it flickered like the portal sparks. Then he began to sew the magical hair into her palm. She winced and jerked back, biting her lip in pain. He held it tight.

"Couldn't you have just given me a ring as well?" she asked through clenched teeth.

"No. You need to be able to read my name to remember it. Don't worry though, I'm almost done."

"Please hurry." She whined.

"I'm trying, but this isn't very easy, you know. I'm not exactly a seamstress and you move a lot."

"You would too if someone was sewing your skin."

"No I wouldn't," he replied matter-of-factly.

Then, when he was finally done, she looked down at her palm to find he hadn't written his name at all, but rather he had just sewn a sun with wavy rays into her skin. The golden shimmer of his hair stood out against the skin of her hand and the little stitches looked just like an embroidery project. She smiled, rather liking the stitches. When he let go of her, she found her hand to be quite heavy and so she used her other hand to help hold it up. A name was a heavy burden indeed.

"It'll get lighter as you go. You'll get used to it."

"Are you sure?"

"No. But I would hope so." He shrugged, then hesitated at a sudden realization. "Have you never taken someone's name before? I thought fae were notorious for that."

"Maybe... maybe not. Perhaps you just have heavy hair."

He smirked and stood up. "Perhaps you're just bad at your job... Be gone. I'll see you soon."

"But where will I find you once I get the beads?" she asked.

But it was in vain. Samas was already gone through a portal, with nothing left but a few sparks and hairs, just as the last time. She sighed and looked down at her hand, touching the sun gingerly and repeating his name out loud so she wouldn't forget it.

~A Jealous Faerie~

Venus left the little cluster of pines, coming back out into the field, which seemed to go on forever. The land stretched up into a tall hill. Sometimes she walked, sometimes she skipped. Sometimes she sat down and smelled the flowers. She went along at her own merry pace, only resting when she grew tired from carrying Samas' name. As she started again, a faerie found her, the tiny kind, no bigger than a sparrow. It flitted to her on the wind. She wore a raspberry as a hat and several magenta rose petals seemed to grow from her skin, clinging to her, and covering her private parts. Her skin sparkled and glimmered in the sun. Six insect wings barely visible in the daylight beat so quickly they hummed. The faerie chirped and whistled like a bird. Any human or creature not of the fae kind would've had no idea what she was saying, but Venus heard the little faerie say hello and ask her what she was doing.

"I'm going to the mountain." She replied, pointing up ahead and finally reaching the top of the hill.

She could see the mountain now, entirely covered in trees save for its peak which was bathed in golden rays. It was nearly a day's walk.

"Why do you journey there?" the faerie asked.

"I need to get to Baba Yaga."

The faerie screamed in alarm, immediately trying to push or pull her back in terror.

"I can't, little one!" Venus replied firmly, then stopped. "I'm bound by my hair."

The faerie stopped and looked at her very sadly, then asked to who.

"I don't know who he actually is…" she realized. "But when I tried to deny the bind, it burnt an entire vineyard. So I have to. I have no choice."

The faerie landed on her shoulder, crying into her hair. Venus covered the faerie with her hand, a sort of comforting hug.

"Run along. I'll be fine. I'll see if the deer will help me get there faster."

The faerie shook her head no, insisting she
accompany her on the journey. To be quite honest,
Venus was grateful for the company. Fae were
social creatures and seldom liked to be alone, even
if they didn't say much. They went along in silence

for a bit. Venus suddenly felt as though someone was walking behind her. She almost turned around to look, then felt whoever come up beside her and brush their arm against her own. She jumped sideways in surprise to find Samas there.

"Samas! I didn't think you'd accompany me anymore!"

"I didn't either but I got bored and you've not found Baba Yaga yet."

"It's only been an hour," Venus replied flatly.

"I get bored easily." Samas shrugged.

The little faerie on Venus' shoulder chirped and squeaked, pointing at Samas as if he weren't right there, blushing profusely.

"Yes, that's him," Venus replied. Samas watched in ignorance, trying to piece together the dialogue by Venus' answers.

"Well, of course, he's quite muscular, he's half monkey half man... Yes, I see that... You want me to what?" Venus rolled her eyes and stopped. Samas stopped beside her.

"She's extremely smitten by you and wants to be given a proper introduction."

"I'd be honored," Samas replied with a humored smile.

"Touah, this is Samas. Samas, this is Touah." She introduced the two.

Samas bowed and held out his finger for her. She took it as though shaking his hand and nearly fainted, her tiny faerie heart beating wildly as she touched his finger.

"It's a pleasure to meet you. Take this hair from my head as a gift." He spoke, plucking a hair and handing it to her.

She took it and squealed, immediately wrapping it around her neck and tying it like a necklace. Samas chuckled. They began walking again. Touah whispered in Venus's ear as if he already couldn't understand her.

"Touah, you know the Queen would never let you. Fae of any kind are only allowed to marry elven men."

Samas snickered. "I can't say I've ever had anyone want to marry me so quickly, least not in a while."

"Do you normally have women wanting to marry you?"

"Well as pri-" Samas began but caught himself, careful not to say too much. "I used to be in a position of authority, back when I was younger. But yes, women of every species always wanted my hand… though mostly for my money. I was almost like a prop."

Touah whispered that she thought it was more likely they wanted him for his body. Venus shook her head and told Samas not to ask what came out of Touah's mouth, as it would just be perverse. He smiled and plucked a couple of grapes from Venus' vines that still grew on her head, popping them in his mouth. He thought to himself how convenient it to always have food on hand, even if it was just grapes. Then, with a twirl of his staff, he took off with a hop into the field. Touah immediately took off into the air, flitting around him as he balanced at the top of the staff, looking out over the trees. Venus took off as well, running after him and doing a few cartwheels and flips of her own. It very quickly turned into a contest of who could do the most in a row but it was quite a ridiculous contest as neither of them really tired.

It ended with a herd of elk interrupting them by running through the open field, their hooves shaking the ground and the wind whipping them in the face as they raced past the two. The elk were a bit different than a normal elk though, as they didn't have antlers, but rather a single horn jutting up from the middle of their sculls, twisting like a gnarled branch. Some looked as though they'd broken off on the end, and others ended with a sharp point. The younglings possessed a small knot on their foreheads like something emerging from underground.

The horned elk never ran into them, all curving around them as swift water around a rock, but Samas grabbed Venus and lifted her to sit atop his shoulder anyway, so she didn't get stepped on. They watched the elk go by, the largest herd either of them had ever seen, full of many young calves.

"Let's join them!" Venus shouted over the thundering stampede.

Samas looked up at her, confused. Venus stood upon his shoulder, looking out at the herd, waiting and timing, then leaped. Samas sprung after her in fright, but for no need. She landed perfectly on the back of one of the elk. He, on the other hand, got headbutted by one and then launched up onto another, using his staff to propel him to not get trampled.

Venus glanced back, laughing at him. "Are you alright?"

He rolled his eyes then moved up to the elk beside her. They rode for several minutes, through field and forest, the wind in their faces as they held on tight with their legs. The elk bounded over rocks and fallen trees and crags in the earth, traversing down a long and steep hill that served as a ramp of sorts, on the outside of a row of rocky cliffs. Eventually, the ground turned to sand and pebbles, opening into a beach of crystal-clear water. The waves broke gently onto the shore as birds called out overhead. The mist of saltwater wafted up their noses.

Venus and Samas hopped off the elk and ran into the ocean water, which the elk waded into to cool off. Samas tackled her, dunking her in the water. She came out with flailing arms, coughing, and sputtering, then doing her best to trip him. It didn't work so she pushed him. He stood firm, not budging and watching her try her hardest. Finally, he decided to tip over, slowly, like a tree falling in the forest. He let her win, much like one lets a child win. He did, however, pull her down with him. She plopped to her knees with a splash. As they sat there in the water, Venus looked up at the cliff to their right. On the top sat a tiny red temple, glistening in the summer sun.

"What's that?"

He turned and saw the little temple. "It's my house. Or at least it's where I've stayed for several years now."

"Where'd you live before that?"

"A palace."

"What palace?"

"You ask a lot of questions you don't need answers to." He pushed her over.

"I just want to know!" she thrashed a bit as she caught herself. "I would never tell anyone else."

"I don't believe that. Fae always tell."

"I don't!"

"And what makes you different?"

Venus opened her mouth to speak but stopped. No words came to mind that she could say to prove him wrong. She took a moment to think. She wasn't any different from any other fae. She wasn't anything special as far as tricks or magic or abilities. She didn't even have her wings yet. She was never boring or a drag, but neither were the other fae. Fae were notorious for flirting and having a good time, especially at the expense of others, no matter the company. She looked down at herself.

"I have your name." she offered, looking down at the golden sun on her palm.

"Yes, that's true. But that's only so you don't forget it." he smiled. "Speaking of questions, why do you wear a crown?"

"Because I'm a princess." She answered, forgetting her own questions.

"How many are there?"

"Easily over a hundred. It's really nothing special to be a princess. Especially if you're the seventy-fifth, like me." She shrugged and swished her hands in the water, blessing it and making it glow blue.

"Well excuse me for my lack of decorum, your highness. If I had known you were royalty, I would've paid you the proper respects." He apologized and took her hand from the water, kissing it dramatically.

As he did, Touah, whom they'd quite forgotten about, finally found them. She bee-lined straight to them, screeching angrily and grabbing Samas' hand, forcing him to let go of Venus. She clamped down and bit Venus on the thumb as hard as she could, drawing blood with her razor-sharp fangs.

"Ouch! Touah! No!"

The little faerie screamed at her in jealousy, sticking her hands on her hips and yelling how dare she be fraternizing with Samas when she knew Touah was head over heels for him. Venus rolled her eyes and sighed in exasperation.

"You don't own him, Touah!" she argued. Samas reached out and plucked the faerie from the air. She immediately calmed down and turned to face him as he held her.

"Touah. I appreciate your affections, but you hurt Venus. And that makes me quite sad."

Touah deflated at the idea of saddening Samas.

"I'm afraid I'll need my hair back."

Touah screamed in protest and grabbed the new necklace protectively.

"I will let you keep it, but only under the condition that you never hurt her again."

Touah glared at Venus and crossed her arms, stomping her feet and throwing a tantrum, but finally nodding in agreement.

"It would never work between us anyways, little faerie." He whispered.

Touah let out a hmph! And flitted off, landing on an elk's horn and sulking. Samas turned back to Venus. He took her hand and looked at the puncture wound from the scorned faerie. The tiny holes were nothing to speak of in terms of size, but they did a wonderful job of puncturing the skin because of their length. Blood now trailed halfway down her forearm. He brought her hand to his mouth, licking the dripping blood from her arm up to her hand and tasting the saltwater mixed with blood as his tongue trailed her skin. He then sucked the puncture wound, spitting the blood out as faeries possess venom. He repeated several times and then asked her if she felt woozy at all.

"A little… but I think only because of you." She confessed.

Samas smirked. Touah watched in jealousy as it happened, then got the idea to fall into the water and pretend to be drowning to get Samas to care for her as well. It went well until she remembered all too late that she couldn't swim and began screaming and thrashing wildly. The elk around her leaned in, sniffing the water and doing no good. Eventually, Venus heard and ran over, picking her out of the water. She held her and gently tapped her back to help her cough up the water while blowing the water droplets off her wings. Touah coughed up the tiniest speck, regained her composure, then turned around. When she saw that it was Venus who had rescued her, she threw another tantrum. Venus rolled her eyes and put her behind her crown to sulk.

"That's quite enough, Touah. You should be ashamed of yourself." She lectured her. "You're acting like a child."

Samas stood and joined them, picking up his staff from the water and twirling it around, the water spraying off it. "I've distracted you too much."

"Hopefully when I see you next, I'll have your beads." She said, turning to him, but he was already gone.

She looked around, trying to find where he'd gone. She sighed, tired of his vanishing acts. In the corner of her eye, she saw something glint in the sunlight. At the top of the cliff, standing on the edge was Samas. In his hand was his staff, the broken bells shimmering in the light. She waved to him, unsure of if he saw her or not. He waved back, then turned and walked away, disappearing over the ledge. Venus decided it was time for her to go, and made her way out of the water, back up the hill and through the trees.

~ *Baba Yaga* ~

After following the tracks of the elk where the ground was torn up and trampled in, she finally returned to the field where the mountain came back into view. Then, the rather unexpected happened. Out from the opposite tree line came a rickety old wooden house, running straight for her on two legs. Its long strides covered an alarming amount of ground with each step. Straw and dirt from the base of the house trailed out from behind it on the wind, and its shutters creaked, one of them slamming open and shut like a wing.

Venus and the faerie screamed at the top of their lungs. Venus instinctively ran away, even though she should have run towards it, her heart pounding and mind racing. Those giant chicken legs ran much faster than her own tiny ones. She normally glided over the grass like she was weightless. Samas' name seemed to slow her down. She ran with her arms sort of crossed, as her hand was too heavy to leave at her side.

She had almost reached the tree line when the front door of the house squealed open and the house itself bent down, scooping her up by the stairs, and flung her inside. The door slammed shut. She rolled across the dirty hardwood floor, being bounced around as the house ran. After a moment of flopping around, she finally got a grip on herself, propping herself up on her hands and knees then grabbing onto a wooden staircase railing with white knuckles. She saw an open window to her right and pushed herself to her feet. She ran over, propelling herself with the momentum of the house. It slammed shut just as she arrived, nearly taking off her fingers. An alarmed squeak came from her mouth. The house seemed to push her back down. She tried for the opposite window and the same happened. She tried the door but it was locked. She sat on the floor, her chest heaving as she clung to the rusted doorknob with one hand and reached up to check on Touah who was now hiding in her hair. The faerie chirped in her ear, letting her know she was okay.

"Look for a way out." Venus breathed as she searched the house for an outlet.

It was empty. Nothing but dust and cobwebs and a wooden table that somehow never moved, inside. The house continued to bounce on, the journey no less comfortable as they climbed the slope. She looked down at her hand now. Samas had turned out to be right though, her hand did seem to be getting lighter. Perhaps it was because she was getting closer to her destination. She looked down at the old floorboards, seeing the blurred ground beneath them through the cracks in the wood as they sped over it. She decided to do nothing but wait on the bumpy ride since there was no way out and it was most likely taking her where she needed to go. Her gut twisted and turned though, the idea of meeting Baba Yaga making her sick. It was too late though, it seemed fate was handing her over on a silver platter.

She bounced around for what seemed like forever but was only an hour. That was far too long in her opinion. Once they arrived, the house slowed down. It descended with a quick drop. The house sat down with a thump. As it did, it spat her out. She rolled on the hard ground, wincing as she was jabbed with tiny rocks and tree roots. As she sat up she found herself in a great forest, the floor being made up of dirt and moss and tiny white flowers.

The smell of pine and sap filled her nostrils, a fresh, invigorating smell. Golden rays peeked through the growth overhead and nothing surrounded them but woods for miles. Touah finally peeked out from behind Venus's crown and looked around, finding the area quite wonderful, or at least until she remembered the house right behind them. Venus didn't recall the door ever shutting behind her, but as she stood up, the door opened again.

"Come in!" a woman's voice called. "What a pleasant surprise. A fae as my guest!"

Venus furrowed her brows in determination. She crept inside. A fire had come to life in the stone hearth and she was now surrounded by bookcases that spilled over with old leather-bound covers and parchment pages. Shelves of herbs and remedies, dried flowers and cast-iron dishes, and various knick-knacks lined the walls. The same giant table sat in the middle of the room and at it, two chairs. Atop sat a mountain of pink yarn and in-progress crochet projects. The house had transformed into something rather chaotic yet welcoming. It was warm to the eyes, but that didn't stop the pit in Venus' stomach. Her soul ached more and more with every second she was inside.

"Welcome, dear fae." Baba Yaga greeted her, acting surprised to see her.

She stooped over the fire, stirring a nice stew that filled the air with savory aromas. A shrimp and cabbage stew. Her favorite. It was just like Baba

Yaga to be making her favorite stew. Her mouth watered. She looked down at her hand, reminding herself of two things; get Samas' beads and never eat from Baba Yaga's table or be cursed forever. She looked back up.

"I came to retrieve something." She began.

"I know." Baba Yaga replied.

The firelight illuminated her wrinkles and sky-blue eyes. Her leathery skin was all too pale for Venus' liking as she could nearly see right through it. Her many layers of draped clothing looked like curtains hanging from a bent rod that were her shoulders.

"Eat first, won't you?" Baba Yaga changed the subject, scooping out a bowl of steaming hot soup and smiling. Her perfect teeth seemed off to Venus compared to the rest of her. She seemed caught somewhere between fiteen and fifty.

"Whose teeth are you wearing?" she asked.

Baba Yaga scoffed, seeing Venus couldn't be tricked all that easily, and tossed the whole bowl of soup in the fire. It burst into flames, blue sparks going everywhere as the spell was burnt. A foul smell of sulfur and suffering came from the fire. She walked over to the table and reached into the mess of yarn to retrieve three silver beads. Venus couldn't help but reach her hand out to snatch them up as soon as her eyes caught the silver twinkle. Baba Yaga smacked her hand away.

"Not so fast! I have a deal to make with you first."

Venus groaned at the thought of another deal. Baba Yaga chuckled as one does when they're in control and twirled the beads in her hand.

"I'll give you the beads if you bring me a peach from Samas' tree. Yes, I read the name on your hand."

"What do you two have against each other?"

"That's not for you to know."

"Then no." Venus folded her arms. "Pick something else."

"No." Baba Yaga replied mockingly, then making a plucking motion in the air, stealing a hair from Venus' head.

It shot through the air and into the witch's hand. Venus launched at her, fed up with having people steal her hair. They both crashed to the ground and rolled around, their hands clutching each other's with white knuckles as they fought over the glowing hair. Baba Yaga proved much stronger than she appeared, despite being nothing but skin and bones. Venus fought as hard as she could, anger rising inside her. As it did, the roots of the surrounding trees felt her anger, and shot out of the earth, coming up around the house and pulling down on it. The house groaned and creaked and rocked, dust falling from the ceiling.

"You fool!" Baba Yaga cackled manically. "I can build a new one with a simple spell."

She bit into Venus' shoulder, drawing blood with her sharp teeth. Venus screamed in pain but refused to let go. Touah emerged, finally mustering up enough courage to help, and dove straight into Baba Yaga's face, sinking her teeth into the witch's cheek. She swatted at her with her free hand. It gave Venus enough time to gain a slight advantage. She pulled as hard as she could, ripping the hair in two. It broke, the glow being snuffed out. Baba Yaga screeched, her eyes reddening as her blood vessels popped in rage. She ignored the tiny faerie flitting around and biting her like an annoying fly, and tackled Venus, grabbing a fistful of hair and ripping it out.

She erupted in victorious laughter once more as she held the clump of silver locks. Venus grabbed her hand and drove them both forward, shoving the hair into the fire and scorching them both. They roared in pain. Baba Yaga recoiled, stumbling backward into a shelf and knocking its contents onto the floor. An unfortunate potion spilled out about her dirty bare feet and she stepped in it. She glanced down, read the label, and laughed.

"Stupid fae." She jeered, watching herself grow three sizes her own and tower over Venus. She stooped over even more as she bent to fit under the ceiling which creaked against her back. Venus stopped breathing altogether for a long moment. Baba Yaga snatched Touah out of the air and crushed her in her fist, killing the fairy. Blood seeped out from between her fingers.

Venus screamed in agony as she felt the light of the little faerie's heart go out. She stumbled backward to the door and tried to escape, but it slammed shut on her once more. Before she could do more, Baba Yaga took one giant step and pinned her down with her foot. Venus fought and squirmed, coughing as she struggled to wiggle out from under her weight. Baba Yaga leaned down and plucked a hair from her head and wrapped it around her finger.

"Now. Get me a peach, you dumb girl."

Venus shoved away as she let her up, running from the house which now let her out, and getting as far away from there as she could. Tears spilled over her eyes and blurred her vision until she couldn't see. The only thing that kept her from tripping was the tree roots sensing her despair and parting to let her through without trouble. She eventually tripped on her own feet, falling and staying down. The trees joined their roots together and lifted her up, passing her gently to each other to help her down the mountain.

Once at the base, they laid her down and hovered over her to give her shade, letting their leaves fall on her in a blanket of green. She cried for herself, but mostly for Touah, her tears creating a small pond around her face. She would've fallen asleep if it weren't for familiar sparking in the air and Samas appearing from a portal in front of her.

"What happened?" he gasped, crouching down and sliding a hand under her head. He found the bald spot and saw her blistered hands and bleeding shoulder.

"She killed Touah… and stole a hair."

Samas' shoulder's sunk at the news. He closed his eyes, tears instantly streaming down his cheeks and into his golden beard at the events which had all come from a choice he had made. Now others were paying the price. He sat there and wept in silence, his throat tightening. He put his other hand over his face, hiding his expression of grief. After a moment of grief and a deep breath, he opened his eyes and wiped his tears away.

"What did she ask of you?"

"A peach from your tree."

He couldn't help but snort, his whole disposition turning from despair to humor.

"Why does she want a peach?" she asked.

"She thinks they give eternal youth. She's just a human using her own spells to stay alive but she thinks that with one of my peaches she could be young forever." He explained.

"What do they actually do?"

"Nothing." He shrugged. "It's just a peach. They do taste good though."

"Why can't she steal one herself?"

"I guard it."

"So what do we do now? I'm bound to her."

"We give her a peach... a poisoned one."

"She'll know! She read my hand before she even saw it." Venus argued.

"Don't worry. This isn't a spell or a bind. We'll use a good old-fashioned winter moth sting. Odorless, tasteless, and completely clear. She won't see it coming." He chirped. "Now let's go to my temple. You can't go back there in your state."

She nodded and pushed herself to a sitting position, feeling quite heavy. He picked her up, and with a mighty leap, took them straight through a portal.

~A Bathtub and A Kiss~

White light swirled all around them in a rainbow, reflecting every color the eye could see and every color they couldn't. Orange sparks fizzed all around, hitting them in the face. They didn't hurt though. Then, as if nothing had even happened, they arrived, standing atop the cliff. In front of them, at the peak of the cliff, stood a strong, young peach tree, its leaves and blossoms quivering in the breeze.

Venus gazed around, taking in a deep breath. Warm sunshine and the song of birds greeted them. To her left was the gradual slope that turned into a grassy plain. To her right was the steep cliff, dropping down into a massive canyon, nearly three thousand feet deep and painted in reds, golds, browns, and even blues. The expanse seemed even wider from up here than it did down on the beach.

Wind blew up from the ocean and sprayed them with a slight mist. Pearlescent and white, fluffy clouds danced in the sky like mantas in the ocean.

"Come inside. Let me fix you up." Samas told her after a moment of enjoying the scenery.

He used his staff to propel himself past the peach tree to the little red temple, snagging a peach as he went. Venus couldn't deny that the peaches were quite beautiful and seemed rather enticing. But even if they did give eternal life, to an immortal like herself who'd never thought twice about it, she couldn't quite understand the yearning to live forever that mortals had.

She followed Samas inside, remembering her bleeding shoulder and throbbing hands. The creaky, abandoned temple ceiling was higher than she could even really see, the top being rather dark as there were no windows up that high. It was simple, being made up of one room with his bed and prayer mat rolled up on one side at the base of the altar. In the center sat a great porcelain tub, which was already filled with water, and an in-ground firepit beside it. Open windows let in the warm wind and long, golden bars of sunlight on the wooden floorboards, revealing the dust that Samas had missed when he swept.

He broke the peach he had plucked in two and gave it to Venus. She took it gingerly in her blistering hands.

"What's this for?" she asked.

"Eating. Aren't you hungry?"

She snorted in laughter and nodded, consuming the peach half much quicker than she thought she would, and then finishing the second half after it. Once done she looked at Samas, who had lit his pipe and was smoking, merely waiting for her to finish eating. He took the pit and tossed it out the window.

"In the tub." He instructed her and nodded to the white tub as he puffed.

"I assume it's just a normal tub for bathing?"

"Get in and find out." He shrugged.

She took a deep breath, hoping it was just a normal tub, despite something telling her it wasn't. She lifted her leg over, stepping in. As she did, Samas made a fake jump at her, scaring her. She let out a startled screech and fell in the tub, splashing water everywhere. Samas tried to hold back his smug laughter but couldn't help himself, his smile giving him away. She splashed him for scaring her, her heart still pounding. His smile disappeared and a frown took its place.

"You put out my pipe." He grumbled, looking at it with disappointment.

"You liar." She fumed. "It's just a bath."

"I'm not a liar. Submerge yourself all the way and really find out." He replied.

"I don't believe you."

He shrugged and swung up to the rafters to fix his pipe. She sighed and sat there for a moment, the water feeling quite fantastic on her burnt hands, then took a deep breath and slipped under the surface. As soon as she did, the walls and bottom of the tub disappeared from beneath her and she floated freely. She jerked in a panic and opened her eyes. She was in the open with nothing around her for miles but water. She thought it might be an illusion, so she paddled forward to swim and go deeper. It wasn't. She moved and swam as though in the ocean. As she went along, she heard a voice.

"Venus! My dear. Look at you. You're a mess... I suppose you're here for healing."

"Mother?" Venus jerked back, ceasing swimming as she recognized the voice.

Goosebumps covered her skin and the water grew cold, chilling her to the bone. Her mother was nowhere to be seen, but her voice surrounded her.

"It's been too long since you've visited my waters, child. And now you visit me in such a state. Who brought you here?"

"I call him Samas." Venus trailed off, realizing she was talking in the water without air or gills.

"Ahh... I've grown very fond of that monkey." The woman's voice chuckled in realization. "He's quite a fickle man... but a good one indeed... how is it you've become entangled in his mistakes?"

"Mother, you know him?" she asked as she floated, looking out into the endless blue expanse.

"Of course, I know him. He comes to my waters often, just to talk, though he's only brought one other to me for healing, and that was a doe. He usually only stays for a few minutes, but sometimes we talk for hours. He gets very lonely all on his own. I'm glad he found you. I wasn't sure he was even going to look for you."

"What's that mean?"

"I told him to find you. I knew you could help him. He did seem a little reluctant and took some convincing though. He doubted the fae but it seems he's figured out not to on his own."

"But why would you tell him that? I'm not a warrior. I've never done anything heroic before."

"Neither have any of my other daughters. Fae aren't really supposed to. But you're the most tenacious. And I named you Venus for a reason. You're the second closest to the sun, or Samas."

"Who is the first?"

"Me of course." Deidra chuckled. "He's become like a son to me. Anyways… I will heal you, not just because you are my daughter, but because I enjoy Samas as well."

Immediately Venus' whole body tingled and itched as Deidra, water goddess and mother of all fae healed her wounds. She inhaled in relief, all the pulsating pain that she'd been ignoring dissipating and washing away. She relaxed, letting herself just hang limp in the water.

"Thank you, mother." She sighed. "Now tell me how you met him."

"He plucked one of my hairs. I must help him now."

"Hmm… Yes, indeed. It's an unfortunate thing… but I'm glad it was him who did the plucking and no one else. I know you will succeed though, Venus. I will bless your journey and give you your first set of wings. You're ready for them… Now be off. He's waiting for you."

Deidra finished speaking and pushed Venus back towards the surface with a current, giving her no options to stick around any longer. Her ability to breathe underwater ceased and she inhaled a nose full of water, her sinuses burning as she choked. The sides and bottoms of the tub reappeared. She grabbed hold and pulled herself back up, gasping for air and coughing up a mouthful of water.

Samas came to her side, hopping down from the rafter and landing in a squat beside the tub. He took her hands, finding them completely restored. Her hair was back to normal as well, and quite unbreakable. He tried to pluck one out but couldn't. Then he noticed, coming from the base of her neck was two small wings, shimmering and iridescent. Venus fluttered them, stretching them out as they unfurled.

"What are those for? There's no way you could actually fly with those."

"Mother gave them to me. They'll help me be lighter on my feet. Eventually, I'll get two more sets."

He let out a thoughtful hum and ran a finger down the length of one of the wings. "When?"

"I don't know. It's different for everyone… I'll never fly as Touah did. But I'll be faster. Anyways. Thank you, Samas. For bringing me here." She smiled at him. "I accept this gift with my friendship. If you'll have it."
He thought for a moment. A smile tugged at the corner of his mouth at the offer.

"I'll accept your friendship… under one condition."

"Why? This can't go in a circle!"

"Why not?"

"It stops here. One thing for one thing. That's how it is."

"I think that's quite stupid. I'll accept your friendship if you give me a kiss." He smiled.
She scoffed. "I'll give you a kiss if you give me my hair back."

"No." he replied all too quickly.

She stood up. He stood up too, kissing her on the mouth. She pushed him away, rather offended. She grabbed for his hand, trying to steal the hair back, but he leaped away, too fast for her to grab.

"Give it back!" she shouted.

"I never agreed to that." He swung away.

"You don't play very fair!" she crossed her arms, watching him swing around. He swooped down, hanging by his legs and dangling his hand just above her reach. She jumped as high as she could, but to no avail. Her wings were too new and not strong enough yet to help her much. She stood and thought for a moment of what she could possibly say to checkmate him.

"You don't deserve my friendship."

He immediately dropped to the ground in front of her, standing up. He stood at least a foot taller than her. He looked down at her, all the playful glimmer gone from his eyes.

"You don't mean that." He said after a while.

She didn't budge, searching his eyes for a clue.

"Take your kiss back. But please leave your friendship."

"Fine." She agreed. She pulled him down to her height, confident in herself until she was there; centimeters from his face, his own eyes fixated on her lips.

"You played me, didn't you?" she whispered, ashamed she'd fallen for such a rouse.

He just smiled a smug, victorious smile.

"Fine. I'll give you a kiss."

She took a shaky breath, leaning in and kissing him gently. Their eyes instinctively fluttered shut. They stayed there for a moment, and then she pulled away. He smiled.

"I can die a happy man now… I've finally been un-kissed by a fae."

She leaned in, surprising him and kissing him again. And again, and again. Each time a little more ardently than the last. Samas grabbed her by the back of the thighs and pulled her body close. Water from her hair dripped down the small of her back. Finally, after several moments of the rather unexpected kiss, they parted; the golden sunlight illuminating each other's skin and revealing little bits of dust floating in the air between them.

"What was that for?"

"I don't know… I've never taken a kiss back before." She admitted.

"Well… I would've thought quite the opposite. But I believe we're uneven now. That was *far* more than what I did."

He regained his composure with a wink and a peck on the cheek, then let go of her, hopping across the room and swinging from a beam like a trapeze. He landed in the open doorway, sitting down on the porch, and looking outside at the setting sun. She followed him, standing at his side. So much had happened and all because of her mother. But somehow, she didn't blame her. It was strange. She started out quite annoyed by Samas, and sometimes she still was, but she figured it might always be that way. Then she thought. Always.

What did she even mean by that? Another thing she didn't understand. But she also enjoyed him tremendously, despite his roping her into this. It was something she then decided to overlook. However, she did want to know more about the whole origin of his predicament.

"What did Baba Yaga take from you? I mean, really take from you."

"My identity. It's why you forgot me right after you met me." He sighed. "I need you to get my beads back. They give me my identity. I can't do it on my own. I would if I could, but I can't even see her to do it because of her spells."

"I'll get them back, Samas." She replied with great resolve. "Will you give me a peach?"

"Only if you give me your name."

She groaned, then sighed. "… Fine. Do you have a needle?"

He shook his head no but plucked one of his own hairs from his head. It was a thin spike from the top that she would have never known was any different had he not shown her. Even sharper than a man-made needle; it worked wonderfully. She plucked one of her own hairs, as only she could do now, and tied it around the spike. She took his hand and sewed the hair into his palm. He didn't wince, just as he had said he wouldn't. He merely sat and watched her sew the hair intently as the sun glowed orange on her skin. Then when she was done, she revealed the silvery planet with a long tail on his palm.

"Venus." He read aloud.

"I've never given anyone my name like this before."

"May I be the first and the last?" he asked.

"Sure."

He beamed. "Now, a peach."

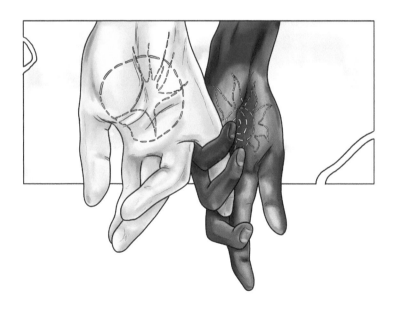

~A Poisoned Peach~

Outside again, they stood under the peach tree. Samas plucked the biggest, ripest, juiciest peach he could find from the branches while Venus called a winter moth. It came on the breeze from the canyon below, living in the cracks and crevices of the sharp rocks. It flitted up to her, its flight pattern quite erratic, landing on her shoulder, then moving to her hand. Fuzzy antennae quivered in the wind and fluttered its white wings to stay in place.

"Hello, friend. Thank you for answering my call. Can you do me one favor? In exchange, I'll bless your offspring for all the generations to come in."

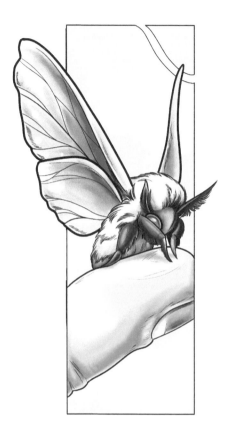

The moth shook its fuzzy head and twitched its fuzzy antennae, moving around a bit and then nodding in agreement. Samas took the moth from her, holding its gently in hand and then giving it a light squeeze. A stinger, smaller than a normal eye could see, shot out from its behind and stung the peach, injecting it with deadly poison. Then, he released it, handing the moth back to Venus. She blessed the insect, its fuzz glowing for a second, and then released it. Samas wrapped the peach in a cloth, tying up the ends with a string and handing it to her.

"I'll take you as far as I know. You'll have to go the rest of the way alone."

She nodded and grabbed onto him. He grabbed his staff from where it leaned on the tree and opened the portal. Once again they were met with a face full of orange sparks and then they were back at the base of the mountain. Venus stared up at it. She could see Baba Yaga's rooftop peeking out from the trees. Smoke wafted up from the chimney and dissipated as it climbed into the sky.

"I'll be waiting right here," Samas said.

Venus took in a deep breath and turned, heading up the mountain. She hopped over crags and crossed fallen trees. Much to her relief, the house met her a few minutes into her walk. It barreled through the forest once again, scooping her up and tossing her inside. She braced herself on the bumpy ride and was once more spit out onto the dirt. Getting spit out onto dirt by a house was no less pleasant the second time than the first. However, this time, she paid it no mind and guarded the peach with her life, careful not to squish it. The old wooden door creaked open, and Baba Yaga's voice came from inside.

"So you came back." she mused.

Venus entered, walking slowly over to the table and setting the parcel down. Baba Yaga turned and clapped her hands together. To Venus' relief, she had returned to her normal height.

"I trust I will find what you are bound to bring here inside? Unscathed?"

Venus nodded, rigid with fear, her heart nearly frozen in her chest. Baba Yaga came over and untied the string, letting the fabric fall about the table. She gasped in amazement at the sight she saw. The beautiful pink and golden fruit seemed to shine on her table even more vibrant than on the mountain. Venus wasn't sure whether to attribute that to the poison or the fact that everything in the house was rather drab and dark. Baba Yaga stared, so entranced with her prize that she didn't even notice the silver hair on her finger breaking as the bargain was fulfilled and Venus was freed from her bond.

"Give me the beads." She spoke.

Baba Yaga ignored her, picking up the peach and smelling it, a wide, euphoric smile plastered on her face.

"The beads!" Venus spoke up, impatient to leave.

The witch continued to ignore her. Venus waited a few seconds. Baba Yaga licked the peach, waited, then bit into it. A giant, juicy bite. The juice dripped down her lips and chin. She waited a bit longer, then took another bite, laughing joyously and then devouring the entire thing in several bites, pit and all. Venus' heart stopped as she saw the age in Baba Yaga seem to reverse, though if she had known better, she would have known it was simply the joy of satisfaction. But she had her chance and she had to take it.

Venus reached out, digging her hand into the pile of yarn and grasping three silver beads in her hand. Baba Yaga finally acknowledged her, reaching out to stop her. Venus yanked her arm back just quick enough, leaping back and grabbing the closest thing to her that could break a window, being a heavy book, and throwing it as she ran. She'd learned her lesson from her previous encounters with the windows. The book shattered the glass of the shutting window. Venus sprang through it and began sprinting down the mountain.

"Give that back, you little thief!" Baba Yaga screamed, careening out of the window after her.

The wild woman chased after her, over bush and rock and tree and moss. Venus' chest heaved as she gripped the beads in her sweating palm, her nails drawing blood from her own hand as she did. She worried that perhaps they had given her the wrong poison or something had gone amiss somehow, despite their plan going exactly as hoped. Perhaps Samas had the wrong species of moth. But as they ran, Baba Yaga closed on her heels. The witch began to vomit. Her body tried to rid itself of the flesh-eating toxin. Her face turned pale and her veins bulged. She screamed in agony as she tripped along. Soon, her legs began to give up and she fell, rolling down the hill and passing Venus along the way. Venus saw her hit the bottom. She crawled to her hands and knees, screaming and coming straight for Samas. She pulled a dagger from her belt and lifted it to strike. Samas didn't even see her.

"Samas!" Venus screamed. "Baba Yaga is right in front of you!"
He looked around but saw nothing, except Venus' wild eyes as she flailed towards him.

"Portal! Now! Jump to me!"
He didn't understand but trusted her anyway. She drew back her arm and flung it forward, throwing the beads into the air. They flew through the sky. Baba Yaga drew back to stab Samas in the chest, driving the nasty, rusted dagger forward. He disappeared into thin air, reappearing in front of Venus just in time. The bells seemed to catch them on their own, fixing themselves with a flash of light and the sweetest, most heavenly tinging Venus had ever heard. Baba Yaga fell down, screaming in agony and covering her ears.

"Noo!!" she wailed, her body now withering away. Her screams filled the air until her body turned into dust floating away with the wind.

As the silver bells fixed themselves, Samas was restored. He was taken up into the air for a moment, his golden hair shimmering in the sun and his once dingy clothing now sparkling brand new. His wooden beads turned to solid gold. When he descended again, a prince's crown of gold and diamonds appeared on his head.

"The Monkey Prince!" Venus gasped, immediately dropping to her knees and bowing before him, recognizing him as the magic disappeared.

He was indeed the monkey prince whom she once admired from afar, the prince who would have been king over every land and species within the faerie realm. How could she have forgotten? She knew it was all due to the spell but it didn't stop her from feeling rather stupid. Samas chuckled and pulled her back up to her feet.

"Don't bow. You're my friend."

"You're supposed to be king! You disappeared before you could even be crowned! The czar took your place! You've been gone for years!" she babbled. "I thought you were dead!"

"I know."

"How?!"

"When I was younger, I was afraid of the responsibilities and duties my position as king would force me into. So I went to Baba Yaga. I asked for a way out. She suggested my identity in exchange for the portals. Being young and naïve I saw no downside. But as time went on I saw the truth. No one knew who I was, no one recognized me. When I tried telling people, they laughed at me. I realized soon that everyone who met me forgot about me minutes after we'd met. I had no identity. I was nobody. When I sought out Baba Yaga to reverse the deal, she hid herself from me. I searched for a long time but it was no good."

"What about the peach tree?"

"I thought there was no way out so I took myself down to the ocean to drown. Deidra refused to let me do so, washing me back to shore every time and giving me the tree as a gift, so I might have a purpose. I enjoyed it for a bit. But it wasn't enough. I was lonely. Then, on that fateful night, I took her advice and found you."

Venus stared at him for a while, taking in everything before she spoke.

"So what will you do now?"

"I'm going to take up my throne. As I should've in the first place."

Venus smiled and looked at the bells tinging gently in the wind. She saw the silver hair on his finger was no longer there. She was free at last.

"May I still have your friendship?" he asked.

She held out her hand with his name still on it. He took it and laced his fingers into hers, then leaned down, touching his forehead to hers. They stayed there, closing their eyes and thinking of nothing. For a moment, nothing else mattered but the wind in their hair, the birds in the sky, and each other. Then she finally spoke.

"A friend is a burden I can carry. No matter how heavy. But now it's my turn to make a condition."

He pulled back in surprise.

"Take me to the vineyard."

He laughed and scooped her up, attempting to take them through a portal and then falling flat on the ground. When he got his beads back the deal had been broken and his ability to teleport taken away. He snorted at the irony and picked Venus back up, propelling away on his staff and taking them to the vineyard.

There, just as he had said, it was already growing back. Bright green leaves sprouted up from the ground and replaced the dead ones which fed them. The earth smelled fresh and rich; her blessing proving to have worked.

Not only a few days later, giant, purple and green grapes, twice the size and sweetness of before, had grown up, winding around the new trellis, and providing Samas and Venus with shade as they strolled through it in the warmth of the afternoon. They did this quite often in the days to follow after Samas had taken his rightful place as king of course, which is his own story and adventure.

They spent their time talking and laughing, chasing each other through the vines. Samas always tried to steal a hair, but only by the power of Deidra never succeeded. One successful endeavor though, was that on many occasions, he stole many kisses from her. And she always took them back. Just as she had in the tiny, red temple. And so, they lived happily ever after, into their next adventures.

The End

Thank you for reading Venus and the
Peach Tree.
The adventure will continue in
Book Two;
Samas and the Spider's Web

CPSIA information can be obtained
at www.ICGtesting.com
Printed in the USA
LVHW070326290322
714678LV00001B/3